THOMAS & FRIENDS

Thomas' Christmas Delivery

Illustrated by Tommy Stubbs

Random House  New York

Thomas the Tank Engine & Friends®

A BRITT ALLCROFT COMPANY PRODUCTION
Based on The Railway Series by The Reverend W Awdry
© 2004 Gullane (Thomas) LLC
Thomas the Tank Engine & Friends and Thomas & Friends are trademarks of Gullane
Entertainment Inc.
Thomas the Tank Engine & Friends is Reg. U.S. Pat. TM Off.
A HIT Entertainment Company

HiT ™
ENTERTAINMENT

"*Puff, puff. Peep, peep.*" Snowflakes were just starting to fall as Thomas climbed the steep hill. It was Christmas Eve and Thomas wanted to be back in his shed with his friends. The engines' stockings were going to be hung soon and Thomas didn't want to miss that. But Thomas was a Really Useful Engine and he had three very important deliveries to make . . . and they could not wait.

First was a freight car full of food to deliver to the Community Hall. All of the Island of Sodor had been invited to come for a big celebration tomorrow, and there had to be enough food for everyone.

When he arrived, there were many people around to help unload. Everyone was in a jolly mood and the work went quickly.

Suddenly there was a shout. Mrs. Kyndley had slipped
on the snowy walk and dropped a bowl of cranberry sauce.
She was not hurt. In fact, she looked very funny covered in
sticky red goo from head to toe. She laughed along with
everyone else.

When she was back on her feet, she walked over to Thomas and gave him a sticky pat. "Merry Christmas, Thomas," she said, and she went inside to clean up.

"We're done!" cried a workman. "Off with you, Thomas. You have a lot to do yet. Merry Christmas!"

"Peep, peep," whistled Thomas, and off he went into the gently falling snow.

His next stop was to the big school on the hill. Some of the children were unable to go home for the holidays, and Thomas had many parcels to deliver so that they wouldn't feel lonely. The snow was coming down a little harder, but he still had plenty of time to get back to the engine shed and go to sleep before Father Christmas came.

When Thomas pulled up near the entrance to the school, some of the teachers came out and helped to organize the unloading of the packages.

The children were having a snowball fight. *Splat!* A red-haired boy in a green coat threw a large snowball that hit Thomas right in the side of his boiler. *"Peeeeeeep!"* Thomas laughed.

Everyone was helping to unload Thomas now, and he waited until the red-haired boy was standing right beside him. Thomas let out a blast of steam. *"Whoosh!"* The steam loosened the snow on Thomas' roof, which slid off and landed right on the red-haired boy's head. "You got me, Thomas!" laughed the boy.

Soon he was off again. This delivery was the most important of all! Thomas had presents to bring to the Children's Hospital in Vicarstown. All of the children were counting on Thomas to make sure that their Christmas was a happy one. The snow was falling much faster now and was starting to get deep in some places. Thomas had to go carefully so as not to get stuck. He kept telling himself, "The children are counting on me. And this will show Father Christmas what a Really Useful Engine I am!" Soon Thomas could see the lights of the hospital through the falling snow.

As he pulled up, there were children at the windows, cheering his arrival. While the doctors and nurses helped to unload all of the parcels, Sir Topham Hatt came out of the hospital and walked right up to Thomas.

"Thomas," said Sir Topham Hatt, "I have a very important job for you. There is a little boy with a broken leg, who lives in the last house before the tunnel to Ballahoo. It is snowing too hard for his mother to come get this toy train. I need you to take this up to his house."

"Of course," peeped Thomas. "I am a Really Useful Engine! But, sir, my stocking wasn't hung before I left. Father Christmas will forget me."

"Nonsense, Thomas," said Sir Topham Hatt. "Father Christmas will be as proud of you as I am."

So Thomas headed off again. By now the wind was howling all around him, and there was so much snow blowing that it was very hard to see. Thomas, for once, wished he had his snowplow as he moved slowly up the track. Suddenly the wind dropped and there was no more snow. He had missed the house altogether and had pulled into the tunnel.

He stopped and started rolling slowly backward until he could see the lights of the house next to the tunnel.

"Peep, peep, peep!" He whistled again and again, afraid he wouldn't be heard over the wind. At last the boy's mother came hurrying from the house, tightly wrapped in a long scarf. Thomas could see the boy in the doorway, waving. "Thank you, Thomas!" he cried. "You are my favorite engine." Then the boy and his mother went back inside and closed the door against the storm.

Slowly, slowly, slowly, Thomas made his way home. He worried that Father Christmas might not be able to find the engine shed in the storm. When he finally got back to the shed, it was very late at night. The Christmas tree was still lit, and all of the engines' stockings, including Thomas', hung in a row.

Thomas was so tired he was asleep in an instant. He dreamed that he had some presents in his stocking when the morning came.

"Good morning, Thomas! Merry Christmas!" peeped Percy. Thomas woke with a start. He looked down. There was his stocking, and there was a note sticking out of it.

Dear Thomas,
    Thank you for being so kind and helpful.
You are a Really Useful Engine.

    The note wasn't signed, but Thomas thought he
knew who it was from.
    Then he looked in his stocking. It was full to the
top of the very thing he wanted most . . . coal!